To all you bright sparks at Moulsham Junior School! K.G

To Violet M.McQ

TWOO TWIT

by Kes Gray and Mary McQuillan

British Library Cataloguing in Publication Data

A catalogue record of this book is available
from the British Library.

ISBN -10: 0340 882107
ISBN -13: 9780340882108

Text copyright © Kes Gray 2006
Illustrations copyright © Mary McQuillan 2006

The right of Kes Gray to be identified as the author
and Mary McQuillan as the illustrator of this Work
has been asserted by them in accordance with
the Copyright, Designs and Patents Act 1988.

First edition published 2006

10 9 8 7 6 5 4 3 2

Published by Hodder Children's Books,
a division of Hodder Headline Limited,
338 Euston Road, London, NW1 3BH

Printed in China

Twoo Twit

Written by
KES GRAY

Illustrated by
MARY McQUILLAN

Hodder Children's Books

A division of Hachette Children's Books

Twoo Twit certainly looked like an owl.
He had the eyes of an owl, the beak of
an owl and the feathers of an owl.
But he had the brains of a greenfly!

'I thought owls were supposed
to be clever,' said the fox cubs.
'They are,' said their mum.
'So why does Twoo Twit keep crashing
into his tree?'
'He keeps forgetting the hole is around
the other side,' said their mum.

'I thought owls were supposed to be wise,'
said the badger pups.
'They are,' said their dad.

'Then why has Twoo Twit just perched
his bottom on that thorn bush?'
'He hasn't learnt about prickles,'
said their dad.

'Aren't owls supposed
to be good at sums?'
asked the leverets.
'Most certainly,' said
the mother hare.

'Then how come Twoo Twit gave the hawk two hundred and fifty blackberries for two beak sharpeners when they were only six blackberries each?' 'Because he's a noodle,' said the mother hare.

SHOP

'He's a dandelion brain,'
said the weasel kittens.

'He's a mushroom bonce,'
said the partridge chicks.

It was true. Twoo Twit was, without doubt, the silliest
collection of feathers ever to take to the sky.

Every night Twoo Twit's mum would wrap some rosehip sandwiches up in a bag and wave Twoo Twit off to night school.

But Twoo Twit never ever went to school.

Sometimes he would fly to the farm
on the hill to play in the hay bales.

Other times he would fly to the brook
and spend an entire night sending
Poohsticks over the weir.

There were lots of places
Twoo Twit liked going.
Not one of them was school.

Tonight he had decided to go to the church tower to
gaze at the twinkly lights of the town. He was hanging
upside down from the bell, happily munching his
sandwiches, when suddenly …

He was shaken to the roots of his feathers.

CLANG CL

CL

Cl

TWOOOOOO...

'What's happening?' he squawked.

DiNG

NG

DONG

Twit!!

'Make it stop!' he screeched.

But it didn't stop. It wouldn't stop.
The clangs kept clinging and clonging
and the dings kept dinging and donging.

Finally, thankfully, after two long, long, ding dong hours,
the church bell stopped ringing and Twoo Twit
stopped wobbling.

With a squeak and a squawk,
Twoo Twit raced back to the forest.

'But couldn't you read the sign?'
said the animals. 'There was
a big sign in the churchyard.'

'Of course I could read the sign,' said Twoo Twit. 'I have better eyesight than all of you.'

'Well if you could read the sign,
tell us what it said then,'
said the magpie chicks.

'Er… it said, THIS IS THE CHURCH,'
guessed Twoo Twit.

'No it didn't,' said the fox cubs.

'THE VICAR LIVES HERE?'
guessed Twoo Twit.

'Nope,' said
the partridge chicks.

'Er... it said, DECENT ORGAN
PLAYER NEEDED,' guessed Twoo Twit.

All the forest children shook their heads.

'It said,
BELL RINGING
CONTEST TONIGHT,'
chuckled the fawns.

'Eight till ten,' giggled
the badger pups.

'Sandwiches provided,'
laughed the weasel kittens.

'You can't read at all, can you?'
hooted the animals.

With the sound of forest laughter ringing in his ears,
Twoo Twit flew home to his mum and dad and hung his
head in shame. He'd never felt such a cuckoo brain before.

The following night a most unusual sound was heard in the forest. It was as loud as a church bell and as clear as a choir solo, but it came from the school.